Dear Parent:
Your child's love of reading starts here!

Every child learns to read in a different way and at his or her own speed. Some go back and forth between reading levels and read favorite books again and again. Others read through each level in order. You can help your young reader improve and become more confident by encouraging his or her own interests and abilities. From books your child reads with you to the first books he or she reads alone, there are I Can Read Books for every stage of reading:

SHARED READING
Basic language, word repetition, and whimsical illustrations, ideal for sharing with your emergent reader

BEGINNING READING
Short sentences, familiar words, and simple concepts for children eager to read on their own

READING WITH HELP
Engaging stories, longer sentences, and language play for developing readers

READING ALONE
Complex plots, challenging vocabulary, and high-interest topics for the independent reader

ADVANCED READING
Short paragraphs, chapters, and exciting themes for the perfect bridge to chapter books

I Can Read Books have introduced children to the joy of reading since 1957. Featuring award-winning authors and illustrators and a fabulous cast of beloved characters, I Can Read Books set the standard for beginning readers.

A lifetime of discovery begins with the magical words "I Can Read!"

Visit www.icanread.com for information
on enriching your child's reading experience.

I Can Read!™

READING
3
ALONE

THE DRINKING GOURD

A Story of the Underground Railroad

by F. N. Monjo
Pictures by Fred Brenner

HarperCollins*Publishers*

For Olivia

HarperCollins®, 🐃®, and I Can Read Book® are trademarks of HarperCollins Publishers.

The Drinking Gourd: A Story of the Underground Railroad Text copyright © 1970 by F. N. Monjo Illustrations copyright © 1970, 1993 by Fred Brenner All rights reserved. No part of this book may be used or reproduced in any manner whatsoever without written permission except in the case of brief quotations embodied in critical articles and reviews. Printed in the United States of America. For information address HarperCollins Children's Books, a division of HarperCollins Publishers, 195 Broadway, New York, NY 10007. www.harpercollinschildrens.com

Library of Congress Cataloging-in-Publication Data

Monjo, F. N.
   The drinking gourd : a story of the underground railroad / by F. N. Monjo ; pictures by Fred Brenner.— Newly illustrated ed.
     p. cm.—(An I can read book)
   Summary: A young boy and his father help a family of slaves escape to freedom via the underground railroad.
   ISBN-10: 0-06-024330-9 (lib. bdg.) — ISBN-13: 978-0-06-024330-2 (lib. bdg.)
   ISBN-10: 0-06-444042-7 (pbk.) — ISBN-13: 978-0-06-444042-4 (pbk.)
   [1. Underground railroad—Fiction.] I. Brenner, Fred, ill. II. Title. III. Series.
PZ7.M75Dr 1993   92-10823
[E]—dc20   CIP
                                               AC

14 15 16 17 18 LP/WOR 50 49 48 47 46 45 44

❖

CONTENTS

Follow the drinking gourd,
Follow the drinking gourd,
For the old man is waiting
  for to carry you to freedom
If you follow the drinking gourd.

When the sun comes back
*   and the first quail calls,*
Follow the drinking gourd,
For the old man is waiting
*   for to carry you to freedom*
If you follow the drinking gourd.

The riverbank will make a very good road,
The dead trees show you the way,
Left foot, peg foot traveling on,
Following the drinking gourd.

The river ends between two hills,
Follow the drinking gourd.
There's another river on the other side,
Follow the drinking gourd.

Where the great big river meets the little river,
Follow the drinking gourd.
The old man is waiting for
*   to carry you to freedom,*
If you follow the drinking gourd.

Chapter One

FISHING IN CHURCH

Tommy Fuller put his right hand
in his pocket.
There was his apple.
Then he put his left hand
in his other pocket.
There was his ball of fishing line.
"Quit wiggling!"
whispered his brother Sam.

9

"Sit up straight!"
whispered his brother Andy.
It was late afternoon.
The three boys were in church.
They had been there all day long.
Mother and Father were downstairs
with Grandmother Dudley
and the rest of the grown-ups.

All the children sat upstairs
in the gallery.
The girls were on one side.
The boys were on the other.

Across the way Tommy saw his sisters—
Helen, Kate, and Rachel.
Tommy took a big bite of his apple.
Then he took three more bites.

Out of the window
he could see a flock of geese
pecking at the grass
on the village green below.

"Let us sing Hymn Two Sixty-three,"
said the minister, Reverend Morse.

14

Everyone stood up. They sang
"Oh, God, our help in ages past,
Our hope for years to come . . ."
Tommy reached for his fishing line.
He tied one end around the apple core.
"You'll be sorry!" said Andy.
Tommy opened the church window
and threw out the apple core.

15

Three geese waddled over
to see what it could be.
A goose picked on the apple core.
"Come *on*, goose!" said Tommy.
The second goose clamped the core
tightly in her wide bill.

Tommy tugged on the line.

The goose rose up into the air.

"Got her!" said Tommy softly.

The goose squawked and fluttered.

She would not let go.

All the other geese hissed

and squawked and cackled too.

They made such a racket

that the noise filled the church.

Everybody stopped singing.

Reverend Morse looked up at the gallery.

"Deacon Fuller," said Reverend Morse,

"I'm afraid it's Thomas again."

Father stamped up into the gallery.

"Thomas Dudley Fuller," he said,

"turn that thing loose!"

Tommy dropped the line.

The goose fluttered to the ground.

17

Father led Tommy out of the church.
"You march straight home, sir,"
said Father, "and go to your room."
Then he went back into the church
and banged the door behind him.

Chapter Two

THE RUNAWAYS

Tommy walked along, thinking of spankings.

It was dark when he reached home.

Tommy could see the evening star.

He went to the barn

to say hello to the horses.

Father had named them

Dan'l Webster and Henry Clay.

Tommy gave them each an apple.

"*You* don't have to be good in church,
do you?" Tommy said.

The horses stamped and snorted.

Tommy saw the hay wagon
piled high with hay.

He wanted to jump from the hayloft
down into all that hay in the wagon.

So up he climbed, into the loft.

"Hi, Dan'l Webster! Hi, Henry Clay!

Look at me!" he hollered.

Then he jumped into the hay wagon.

Two hens squawked.

Something in the dim loft said, "A-a-a-anh!"

It sounded like a baby crying.

"Who's there?" said Tommy.

Dan'l Webster stamped his hoof.
Tommy climbed back into the loft
to see what had made the noise.
"Who's there?" Tommy hollered.
"Stop right there!" said a deep voice.
"You won't take us alive!"
A black man stood up, covered with hay.
He had an axe in his hand.

23

Tommy was so frightened
he fell back into the hay.
"Oh, my goodness, Vinnie,"
said the man. "It's only a little boy."

24

The man dropped the axe he held.
"We just hiding," he said, smiling.
"We won't hurt you."
"Does Father know you're here?"
said Tommy. "What—
what are you doing in our barn?"

"Is Deacon Fuller your daddy?"

Tommy nodded his head.

"He hid us here," said the man.

A little boy stood up beside him.

"That's my boy Little Jeff,"

said the man. "I'm *Big* Jeff.

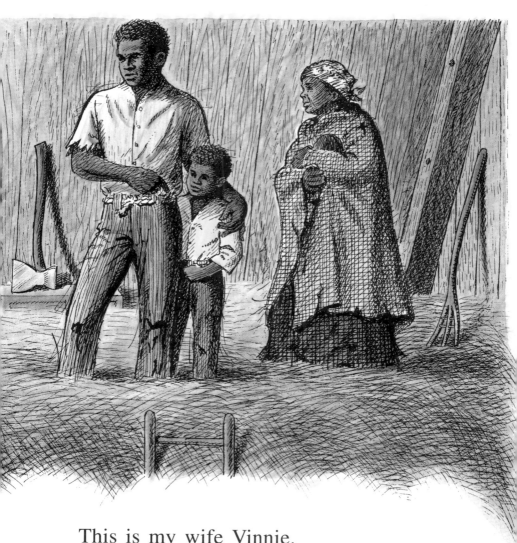

This is my wife Vinnie.

And this is Baby Pearl.

We running away!"

"Running away?" said Tommy.

"We going to Canada," said Vinnie.

"We up from Carolina," said Jeff.

"We been following the drinking gourd
every step of the way."

"The drinking gourd?" said Tommy.

"What's that?"

"Shoot, boy!" said Little Jeff.

"You mean you never heard of the
drinking gourd? I'll show you."

Little Jeff jumped down from the loft
and ran to the barn door.

Up in the wintry sky shone the stars.

Little Jeff pointed to the Big Dipper,
caught in the branches of an elm.

"*That's* the drinking gourd!"

"No, that's the Big Dipper," said Tommy.

"Same thing!" said Little Jeff.

"The front end of the drinking gourd
points straight up to the North Star.
Follow the North Star, and you get to Canada.
Get to Canada, and you be free!"

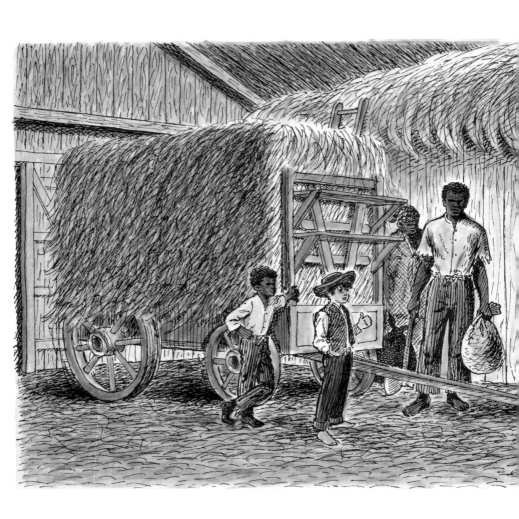

"Thomas Dudley Fuller!" said Father
from the shadows. "Didn't I tell you
to wait in your room?"

"Father!" said Tommy, surprised.

"I—I found Jeff and Vinnie and—"

"I see who you found.

You found all my passengers," said Father.

"Don't ask any questions.

Help hitch up the horses.

We've got to get started."

31

Chapter Three

ON THE UNDERGROUND RAILROAD

Tommy and Father sat in the wagon.
Jeff and Vinnie and Little Jeff
and Baby Pearl were hidden in the hay.
They were driving toward the river.
"I been a slave all my life, Tommy,"
said Jeff, sitting up in the hay,
"until two weeks ago.
That was the day I decided

we would run away to Canada
on the underground railroad."
"The underground railroad?" said Tommy.
"Shoot, boy!" said Little Jeff.
"You never heard about *that* neither?"

"You see, Tommy," said Father,
"the underground railroad isn't
a *real* railroad with steam engines
and tracks and cars.
It's a secret group of people
who believe slavery is wicked.
They live in homes and farms like ours,

stretching from here to Canada.
Everybody in the group
hides people like Jeff and Vinnie,
helping them get away."
"And they got *stations* on the
underground railroad," said Little Jeff.
"Like our barn!" said Tommy.

"And they got *conductors*," said Jeff.

"Like me!" said Father.

"And they got passengers!" said Vinnie.

"Like *us*!" said Little Jeff.

"They call it underground," said Father, "because it's a secret.

Every bit of it *has* to be a secret!"

"You right," said Jeff. "We valuable property. My old master lost $2,500 when he lost us, if he lost a penny."

"Then I'm sure he'll send some men to try to catch you," said Father. "So you get back down under that hay."

"Nobody's going to catch me," said Jeff, "as long as I got my axe."

Then Jeff and Vinnie and Little Jeff and Baby Pearl all hid from sight.

REWARD

Ran away from his Master, Maynard Reeves Bond, of Larkspur Plantation on the Edisto River, Dorchester County, South Carolina, a black fellow about 30 years of age, named Jeff, 6 Feet two inches high, wearing a brown wool jacket and denim breeches. Last seen hereabouts on October 15, 1851. Accompanying the runaway are his wife, Lavinia, age 28, and two children, Jeff, 9, and Pearl, 1. Whoever shall take up these four runaways and return them to their abovesaid Master shall have $250.00 reward. All Masters of Vessels and others are hereby cautioned against concealing or carrying off said Servants, on Penalty of the Law.

Charleston, S.C., Oct. 21, 1851.

"Tommy," said Father,
"don't say a word to *anybody*
about what happened tonight.
Jeff's a brave man.
I'd hate to see a brave man
sent back into slavery. Promise?"
"I promise," said Tommy.

"Whoa, horses," said Father.
"This is the end of the line.
I have to find the boat now.
It's hidden here on the riverbank."
Father walked into the darkness.
A whippoorwill called.

Chapter Four

THE SEARCHING PARTY

Tommy heard hoofbeats on the road.

He saw lanterns bobbing.

Four men on horseback rode up

to the wagon and stopped.

The men got down from their horses.

"Say, young fellow," said the leader,

"I'm a U.S. marshal. These are my men.

We're going to search that wagon.
We're looking for runaways."

"Runaways?" said Tommy.

"A Negro slave," said the marshal,
"his wife, and two children.

"There's a reward for them.
You wouldn't have them hidden
in that wagon, would you, boy?"
Tommy's mouth was dry.

"You won't find anything but *hay*
in this wagon," he said.
"Mebbe we better search it anyway,"
said the marshal.

Tommy was scared.

He thought about Little Jeff

and the others hidden in the hay.

If the marshal found them,
he would send them back down South!
They would have to be slaves!
They would *never* be free!

"Marshal," said Tommy, "I guess
I better tell you all about it.
You see, I'm Tommy Fuller,
and I'm running away myself."
"You Deacon Fuller's boy?"
said the marshal.
"That's right," said Tommy.
"Pshaw!" said the marshal.
"This is the boy made all that fuss
in church this afternoon.
Fishing for *geese*!"

All the men laughed.

"Father was boiling mad," said Tommy.

"He was going to give me a licking.
So I ran away."

"We're chasing the wrong wagon, boys,"
said the marshal.

"You better go home to your pa, Tommy,
and take your licking."

"Yes, sir," said Tommy.

"And next time you go fishing,"
said the marshal, "tell your pa

I want you to catch me two ducks
and a nice fat turkey.
That's an order."
All the men laughed.
Then they rode away.

Chapter Five

OVER THE RIVER

Father came out of the shadows.

Jeff and Vinnie sat up in the hay.

Jeff's axe was still in his hand.

"Tommy, you did just fine," said Father.

"I thought the marshal would find us

sure enough this time," said Jeff.

Tommy was too scared to speak.

"Take the wagon back alone, Tommy,"
said Father. "We have to row
across to the next station."

Little Jeff jumped into the boat.
Jeff jumped in too. He helped Vinnie
and Baby Pearl get settled.
A whippoorwill called.

Father started rowing away.

Tommy heard the dip and splash

of the oars in the water.

"Good-bye, Little Jeff," Tommy whispered.

"Good-bye," whispered Little Jeff.

"Good-bye," whispered Jeff and Vinnie.

Father rowed into the darkness,
and then the boat was gone.

Chapter Six

THE LAWBREAKERS

It was late when Tommy got home.

Everyone was asleep but Mother.

She gave Tommy some supper.

"Is Father all right?" said Mother.

Tommy told her what had happened.

Then she sent him up to bed.

But Tommy stayed awake,
waiting for Father to come home.
He heard the front door slam.
Then Father came up to his room.

"Tommy," said Father,
"I believe in obeying the law.
But you and I *broke* the law tonight.
The law says we were wrong
to help Jeff and Vinnie get away."

"I know Father," said Tommy.

"But can't you *change* the law?"

"I've been trying," said Father.

"We've been trying for years and years.

Someday it *will* be changed.

"But right now the law says
Jeff and Vinnie are another man's property—
property same as a horse or a cow,
property worth $2,500."
"But Jeff and Vinnie are *people*,"
said Tommy.

"Yes," said Father. "That's why
I can't obey that law.
That's why I hate it.
It's *wrong*!"
Then he kissed his son good night
and closed the door.

Tommy lay in bed, thinking about
Little Jeff and the others.
"If they just get to Canada,"
he whispered, "they can be free. . . ."
Out of his window he could see
the bright North Star.
And pointing up to it,
in the dark night sky,
sparkled the drinking gourd.

AUTHOR'S NOTE

This story really could have happened.

In the years before the Civil War thousands of slaves—perhaps as many as 75,000—escaped to freedom, traveling on the "underground railroad." Often they crossed the border into Canada, where they could not be captured by U.S. marshals and forced to return to slavery.

Some of the escaping slaves sang "Follow the Drinking Gourd," a song expressing their fierce need for freedom.

In the free states north of Maryland and the Ohio River, it was against the law to own slaves. Many Americans living there hated slavery. Some of them joined societies that worked to abolish slavery. The members were called *abolitionists*.

In 1850 the Fugitive Slave Law was passed by Congress. It required "all good citizens" to help Federal marshals return captured runaway slaves to their masters. In the North, many people refused to obey that law, just as Deacon Fuller does in this story. And between 1863 and 1865—during and just after the Civil War—slavery finally came to an end everywhere in this country.